Steff Grows an Apple

W9-ATA-533

by David Webb
illustrated by Nan Brooks

Copyright © by Harcourt, Inc.

All rights reserved. No part of this publication may be reproduced or transmitted in any form or by any means, electronic or mechanical, including photocopy, recording, or any information storage and retrieval system, without permission in writing from the publisher.

Requests for permission to make copies of any part of the work should be mailed to the following address: School Permissions, Harcourt, Inc., 6277 Sea Harbor Drive, Orlando, Florida 32887-6777.

HARCOURT and the Harcourt Logo are trademarks of Harcourt, Inc.

Printed in the United States of America

ISBN 0-15-317197-9 – Steff Grows an Apple

Ordering Options
ISBN 0-15-318584-8 (Package of 5)
ISBN 0-15-316985-0 (Grade 1 Package)

2 3 4 5 6 7 8 9 10 179 02 01 00

Steff says apples are good
for people to eat. She is
always snacking on them.

1

One day Steff made some
apple cookies with Dad.
Then she said, "I would
like to keep these."

2

"Why?" asked Dad. "What will you make with them?" "I will grow apple trees," Steff said.

3

"The trees will start to grow
in here," Steff said. "Then I
will put them in the yard."

4

"I will plant them by the barn, and watch them grow."

"What a smart thing to
do," said Dad.
"When will my trees grow
apples?" asked Steff.

6

"Give your trees some
time," said Dad. "They will
grow, but they will not have
apples for a long time."

"Then I will eat these
apple cookies for now!"
said Steff.

Teacher/Family Member ·····································

Apple Book
Cut a large apple shape from red paper. Let your child dictate sentences about growing, cooking, or eating apples. Write the sentences on the paper apple.

School-Home Connection
Ask your child to read *Steff Grows an Apple* to you. Then ask what reasons Steff may have for wanting to grow apples.

Word Count: 124

Vocabulary Words:
says	keep
people	these
always	by
make	give
made	

Phonic Elements: *R*-Controlled Vowel: /är/*ar*
start
yard
barn
smart
Consonant: /y/*y*
yard

···

TAKE-HOME BOOK
Bright Ideas
Use with "Market Day" and "Carmen's Star."